Enchanted

Fairy Tales for Young and Old

Shirl Knobloch

. . .

Enchanted: Fairy Tales for Young and Old

© Shirley Knobloch, 2016

Edited by: Jennifer Sabatelli

Cover and Artwork by: Shirl Knobloch

ISBN 13: 978-0-9974752-6-5

• • •

Also By Shirl Knobloch:

*Birdsong, Barks, and Banter: Adventures of an Animal
Intuitive Reiki Master and Her Home of Misfit Companions*

The Returning Ones: A Medium's Memoirs

You're Never Too Old for Fairy Tales

*Reenactments from My Heart: Spiritual and Supernatural
Civil War Fiction and Poetry*

Once Upon a Fairy Tale

*Strength of a Lion, Soul of a Lamb: A Collection of
Wolfhound Fairy Tales and Poetry*

My Ten Legged Journey: The Road to Rainbow Bridge

*Waiting for the Next Village Attack:
Growing Up Italian, a Jersey Girl Reminisces*

• • •

During the writing of this fairy tale collection, I lost a most dear and treasured friend. My faithful Casper, a beautiful white collie, crossed to Rainbow Bridge at just eight years of age. I wanted to write a special fairy tale for him and created "Spun Gold" in remembrance. I hope my words do just a smidgeon of justice to the gentle and faithful being beside whom I was fortunate to spend eight years of life.

"If I'm honest I have to tell you I still read fairy-tales and I like them best of all." --Audrey Hepburn

Me too, Audrey, me too.

• • •

• • •

Table of Contents

• • •

• • •

Prologue

As I child, I devoured fairy tales. I never imagined that one day I would be the writer of now my fourth fairy tale book. Hearing from readers of all ages has inspired me to compile this latest collection. Within these pages, woodland beings and beings of the sea and sky bring messages of love, compassion, and magick to hearts of every age.

A Lock of Love

Serena was a beautiful young maiden with raven hair and amber eyes. She would wander the slopes of her mountain village, being one with all the creatures of the woods and pastures of her homeland.

Serena had secrets. She possessed gifts only shared among the other beings of the forest, especially the wolves. She did not fear them; they were her friends. One she-wolf in particular moved by her side in the shadows. She was always there guarding the beautiful maiden, making sure no harm came to her. Serena called her Petra, and through the seasons, a bond was forged between mortal and wolf that few humans would ever understand.

One spring, Petra brought a surprise to Serena—three whimpering little pups, all the color of their mother, with amber eyes that mirrored Serena's. One little male had an unusual tuft of white fur on his forehead. "I shall call you Cloud," whispered Serena as she held the wriggling pup to her face. "Your wisps of white fur remind me of the clouds in the sky."

Weeks passed, and Serena watched them grow. Then, fear came to her village. In the night, two of the shepherd's sheep were attacked and killed. This was not a good omen for

Petra and her babies. Serena knew the village men would be coming, armed with guns to kill any wolf in sight.

Serena ran off into the woods to warn her friends. She searched and called, but it was too late. She found them, huddled together, fear in their eyes and blood on their fur. "Oh no," she cried. "My dearest friends!" She embraced little Cloud in her arms and kissed his white tuft of fur.

She pulled a little strand from the top of his still head and opened a gold locket she wore around her neck. She placed the lock of cloud-like fuzz inside and clamped the clasp shut. "I will keep you near my heart forever, little boy," she promised. Serena covered her friends with branches and leaves and placed flower blossoms on their grave.

She didn't go into the woods as much anymore. A beautiful maiden wasn't safe in such a place, especially without her dear guardian's protection. But sometimes, necessary chores beckoned her to wander alone among the forest.

With mushroom and herb basket in hand, Serena set out one beautiful day. Wisps of white clouds floated in the blue sky above her head. "Like you, my friend," she whispered, as she clutched the golden locket at her heart. When her basket was heavily laden, Serena set off toward home.

But danger lurked along the path. Several men had been watching this beautiful, young girl and sprung out from the bushes, blocking her path.

"What is such a beauty doing here in the forest?" one asked, with a wide grin across his face.

"What treasures are in your basket, or elsewhere?" another asked. Suddenly, he grabbed the locket's chain at her throat and pulled it, breaking the golden links. "What have we here?" he asked. "A lover's portrait perhaps? I can be your handsome lover," he whispered.

With that, he opened the locket, sending the wisps of fur at his feet.

"What is it?" the others asked.

"Just some mangy old fur. Useless trash!" he muttered and tossed the locket to the ground. As Serena bent to retrieve it, he grasped her hand tightly.

Suddenly, a whirl of wind began to rise from the ground. A large, white wolf seemed to manifest from the wind itself. He lunged at the men, clawing and attacking them and sending them off running into the forest. Then, with amber eyes glowing, he turned to Serena and gazed into her eyes. "My Cloud," she cried.

In an instant, he was gone. Serena bent down to pick up her locket and found the little tuft of white fur inside. She

clamped the clasp and placed it upon her heart. "My Cloud,"
she whispered once more.

Robin Red Breast

*M*any centuries ago, a little bird dwelled in a place where the sun sweltered in the sky. Life was hard, but the tiny bird scraped the dry, brown clay ground, which resembled the color of his feathers. He foraged for bugs and pecked at crumbs dropped by people in the village.

The songbird loved a little boy in this village. Deep within his heart, the tiny bird remembered a moment of intense pain. It was during that pain that the hands of this boy lifted him close to his own heart and took all the hurt away.

He watched this little boy grow into a man. He sat in the trees listening to him speak. He perched on the Temple roof listening to his voice echo throughout the halls. He followed him to the river as another placed his head beneath the water and baptized him with prayer.

He slept in the eaves of his house and listened to this young man's mother cry with worry and grief. He sang with sorrow as the whip slashed the man's back in painful gashes and remembered his own pain again on that day long ago. He remembered when he was a young bird, lifted into the hands of kindness and healing.

He soared through the dark, sunless sky as the man walked under the weight of a heavy cross to a hillside. He watched as others nailed this man to this cross. His heart cried out as the man's head slumped low and blood dripped from his hands, side, and feet.

His tiny feet perched upon this cross, and he spread his wings apart. Mournfully, he placed his heart against the hand that saved his own heart so long before. And his heart beat so deeply of love and sorrow that his blood rose to the surface of his chest and changed its plumage to scarlet red.

For the rest of his days, his brown feathers would bear a red breast. Forever more, those of his kind that followed after the final beating of his sorrowful, tiny heart would bear the mark of love and passion and gratitude for the one who healed his own heart.

(This fairy tale is based on the story of how Jesus healed a dying little bird as his mother, Mary, watched.)

Spun Gold

--For Casper--

You looked at me as though the sun rose in my eyes.

Now the moon sets in my heart.

Once upon a time, in a land of towers and turrets, there lived a beautiful collie called Casper. Each day, Casper helped herd his master's sheep through the heather. Each night, he laid his gentle body by the hearth for warmth. It was a life without wealth, but not without riches, for the kind master loved the gentle collie with all his heart.

Each night, as his master slept, the wee folk visited the farmhouse. They loved Casper. Gentle as a lamb, they snipped tufts of fur from his body to spin on tiny spinning wheels. Casper's fur kept their wee ones warm throughout the damp, chilly nights of winter. It wrapped their babies in blankets soft as thistle down. Casper never hurt them, allowing the gentle pulling and tugging to go on until the morning sun lifted her golden head in the sky.

Years passed. It was getting harder for Casper to climb the highlands. The chilly rain seeped into his aching bones. He herded less and slept more and more by the hearth. But the man loved him just as much. And the wee folk loved him even more. His fur was sparser now, but being more than enough, he kindly shared with his friends.

The wee folk had much knowledge of the highlands. They knew which herbs to pick, which poultice to apply for bones that creaked, and which balms to soothe a painful paw. Each night, they rubbed Casper's joints and paws and eased his pain. But balms and poultices don't work forever, and Casper grew more tired and weak with each passing day.

One night, the wee folk slipped through the door crack and found him lying very still by the fire. Too still. They knew their friend had gone. As the moon hung sadly in the sky, they went about the task of bidding him farewell. Heather was carried in and placed about his body. The scented perfume of flower nectar was rubbed upon his paws. A basket of golden coins was placed at the foot of the hearth. "Thank you, dear friend," they cried.

From his bedroom, the shepherd heard a tiny wail. Thinking it was Casper, he got up from his bed and went to the hearth. He thought he saw tiny shadows flickering fast about the room and heading for the cracks and corners. "It must be my aging eyes," he thought to himself.

Then, he saw the glistening of coins and smelled the sweet perfume of scented oils in the air. And he looked upon the body of his friend, his fur brushed neatly. Every strand, every knot, neatly lay in place. No matting, no dirt, no tangles.

His old boy looked more handsome than he had ever seen. For such a boy as Casper deserved to travel to the heathered fields beyond in grand fashion. Such was the way of the wee folk; such was the way of farewell to a friend.

The coins were a much-needed blessing for the elderly shepherd. They would see him through his final autumns and winters. But he set one coin aside to bring to the stone maker in the village.

"I wish a beautiful cross to be placed upon a grave," he said. "It will mark the spot of a gentle and faithful friend."

Many years have passed. That stone cross has been chipped and weathered by the harsh highland winds. Though barely legible, the word *Casper* can be seen if a passerby looks closely. Near it, another grave graces the field. Together, the shepherd and his boy lay in final peace together, and heather and scented blossoms cover the ground above. The wee folk see to that.

Forget Me Not

Once upon a time, on a hillside dotted with forget-me-not flowers, lived a majestic, old oak. She towered tall and strong against the wind, her leaves green and glossy amidst her countless branches.

Inside her trunk lived a family of squirrels. Beneath her lived a family of moles. Amongst her branches, the nests of sparrows, cardinals, and blackbirds lay sheltered from the rain. Woodpeckers pecked at her trunk, caterpillars crawled on her bark-laden arms, and hawks perched on her tallest branch to oversee the land.

But she was not well. She could feel her bark separating and weakening under the woodpecker's relentless beak. She could feel her roots struggling to quench their thirst. Her leaves were wrinkling on the edges and losing their sheen to a duller shade of brown.

She was a kind, old oak. So many lives depended on her. At night, she cried with worry for them, and sticky sap flowed down her trunk. "You must leave me," she whispered to the tiny birds that nestled in her arms. "Soon you must find another home," she pleaded to mama and papa squirrel.

But the birds and the squirrels would not leave her. She was their friend. Besides, winter was coming, and finding another trunk to nest in would be difficult for a squirrel family.

Nesting material was sparse; it was too late in the season for tiny songbirds to build new homes.

Each night, the oak cried tears of sap. "Please," she whispered to papa squirrel. "Before my leaves all shrivel, chew them off for the tiny birds to weave inside their nests. My dying branches will not shield them well from the coming winter storms."

"Take some to insulate your nest in my trunk, too," she added. "It will be strong enough for you to brave the winter winds one final season, I promise."

Papa squirrel did as the oak asked. He stuffed leaf after leaf in his mouth and ran across the branches, delivering mouth loads to each tiny songbird. He stuffed the trunk with leaves and moss and mud and covered the hollow to block the wind.

"Thank you," said the oak. She was very barren now; no green leaves graced her branches. Her trunk was peeling, and pieces of it fell to her roots, carried off by the mole family for winter nourishment. Even her tears of sap brought nourishment to the little caterpillars before their dormant rest.

Winter came. The birds slept in their warm nests. The squirrels hunkered down in comfort. The moles slept soundly, only waking to munch and fill their tiny bellies.

When spring arrived, park employees came with chainsaws to fell the giant. The songbirds were out searching for new nesting materials. The squirrels were out foraging for the choicest greens of new spring growth. The moles had burrowed to fresh spring quarters. The caterpillars were spinning cocoons to turn into beautiful butterflies.

The workers cut quickly. One by one, her branches fell to the ground. Pieces of straw and shriveled leaves fell to the ground with each branch. Next, her trunk was sliced in many sections, revealing the countless rings of compassionate years she had given to so many lives. She was hauled away; only sawdust remained to mark the place where her beauty had shadowed the sun.

Soon, the forget-me-nots bloomed again. She was not forgotten. The birds remembered her, bringing their spring babies to tell stories of their friend and show where their homes once stood. The squirrels remembered her, hiding acorns across the hillside where the blue and yellow blossoms bloomed.

Some of those acorns grew up to be oaks. The ancient oak would have loved that. Perhaps she is still there, her energy spread out amongst the forget-me-nots, her roots containing memories of decades of friends and winters and springs. Perhaps she looks down and sees the birds, the squirrels, and the caterpillars and smiles from a hillside in another realm, where her only tears are tears of joy, not sorrow.

Not many humans walk by the masses of forget-me-nots in the park and know her story. But each little being that has lived among the flowers on the hillside will never forget the kind, old tree.

A Dandelion or a Rose

If you had the choice
If fate in your power
Which bloom would you pick:
The weed or the flower?

To fragrance the wind
With scent and allure
Or face life unwanted
By most, I am sure

To walk down the aisle
In bridal bouquet
Or lay in the curbside
With roots tossed astray

Which one would you fancy?
Which one would you choose?
To rise with the sun
Under moonlight to snooze

The rose with the thorns
The weed soft as snow

One fragile as moments

One strengthened by woe

For all love the rose

But few love the weed

She is hated and cut

Before she can seed

But if she survives

Long days of July

Her beauty in nature

No one can defy

For unlike the rose

Whose petals droop down

The dandelion rises

With seeds soft as down

Her beauty soars high

Through the winds and the clouds

As she looks upon rose

Her petals now shrouds

Of brown withered blossoms

Never seeing the sky

That a weed now caresses

Before she will die

So choose one

But choose wisely

The rose or the weed

A moment of beauty

A voyage of seed

Will you stay where you're planted

And wither and fade?

Or soar on the breeze

Once goodbye you have bade?

To the sun

And the moonlight

And summer and sky

Live a life in the journey

Or take root 'til you die.

The Well of Youth

Once upon a time, a farmer and his wife dwelled in a humble cottage among the moors. The land was harsh, and sickness had taken all of their children. One day, a fairy visited the farmer's wife and told her of a magic well. If she drank from this well, she would live forever.

"And what price shall I pay in return?" the woman asked.

"No price in money, dear woman" the fairy whispered. "But you must never share this place with another soul."

"My husband, shall I not tell my husband?" she asked.

"No, not a soul. Remember these words."

The woman followed as the fairy hovered over a cairn of rocks. "Under these stones flow the waters of immortality." With that, the fairy vanished.

Frightened but curious, the woman removed the stones. A deep chasm appeared—an ancient well. A rope hung down, attached to the top wall. Slowly, the woman hoisted up the rope, and a cup brimming full of sparkling water surfaced.

She drank. With each sip, she felt more refreshed, more youthful. She covered the rocks back over and ran home.

"My, don't you look happy!" said her husband. He noticed the rosy tinge to her cheeks and the spring in her steps. He tipped his tweed cap and nodded his head. "What is the cause of this?" he questioned.

"Just the brisk air," replied his wife.

This went on for months. The wife's health improved, but her husband's declined. She wanted to share her treasure with him, but she remembered the fairy's words. *What if she told and the well disappeared* she thought to herself. She craved her renewed beauty and youthful body, craved them too much to risk losing them. And so she kept her secret.

Her husband grew ill. He lay bedridden, too ill to carry on the farm chores. But she had strength for the two of them. Then, she thought to herself, *I am young and pretty again. Why need I struggle doing hard labor at this farm?* So she left for the village.

Men fancied her beauty; woman envied her youth. Each day, she traveled to the well and quenched her thirst from the magic cup. No one in the village recognized her. She wasn't the old farmer's wife anymore; she was a fair young maiden.

Soon, she fell in love with a rich merchant's son. He asked for her hand in marriage, and she accepted, not revealing the dying husband who waited at the humble cottage on the moor.

● ● ●

The couple had a child. A beautiful baby girl with hair the color of gold and cheeks as pink as rosebuds. She was the apple of her mother's eye. But soon, the baby's health declined. Terrified, her mother knew what she had to do. She convinced herself that all would be well. This was not breaking her promise; she was telling no one. Her baby could not speak, so she could not reveal the truth of this charade of youth and beauty.

She swaddled the baby in blankets and set out for the well. She removed the stones and hoisted the cup up from the bottom. She carefully lifted the cup up to her daughter's lips and let the cool water enter her mouth. The baby's cheeks grew rosier, her dull eyes brightened, and her incessant cough disappeared.

The woman hurried home, but her legs ached in an oddly familiar way. She reached the door to her fine home and was met with a scowl on her husband's face.

"Who are you? Where is my wife? Hand my daughter to me now, old hag!"

The woman glanced at the window and saw her reflection in the glass. She was the old hag, the farmer's wife, all youth and beauty gone.

Her heart broken, the woman had no choice but to leave her baby and new husband and wander back out on the moors. She came to the humble cottage and found it empty.

She walked across the moors to the old well and saw a handsome young man walking past on the path. He was handsome, with a sparkle in his eye and a healthful bronze to his skin.

"Good afternoon," he muttered and quickly vanished from sight.

And vanished was the well. All that lay under the pile of stones was a tweed cap, an oddly familiar tweed cap.

Tora Lora Lora

a kind, old man lived alone in a tiny cottage in the Irish woods. His eyesight was fading, but his hearing was sharp as a tack.

One day, a little sparrow high up in the tree outside his bedroom window started singing. Her tune sounded familiar. *Why, that's the song my mother sang to me, "Tora Lora Lora,"* he thought. But it couldn't be, could it? What sparrow knows "Tora Lora Lora"?

Each day, the little bird would come. Each day, her song would be the same haunting refrain from the old man's childhood.

The old man had little, but what he had, he shared with the sparrow. Soon, she was alighting by his feet, pecking at crumbs of soda bread. Then, she started following him around the cottage yard, until one morning, she stepped right inside. And there she stayed. Each night, she sang the man to sleep with her lullaby. Each morning, he awoke to her song. His days weren't as lonely anymore.

Then, one morning, the house was quiet. Quite worried, the old man started looking for his friend. His eyes weren't strong; he was afraid he would step on her by accident if she had fallen or gotten hurt.

Then he saw her. She was breathing very shallow, her song very still. He cradled her in his arms and started crying. Suddenly, she flew out of his arms toward the sunny window.

"What is wrong, dear one?" he asked. "Is it time for you to leave?" The sunlight's glare hurt his eyes. The light was suddenly very, very bright.

"Yes," a familiar voice answered. "But do not cry. I am not leaving you. It is time for me to go, but not alone, my son. I have come to take you home with me. It is time we both left for heaven."

The old man felt his body light as air; suddenly, he was soaring through the clouds. Ahead of him was his mother, a beautiful winged Angel, singing "Tora Lora Lora."

Falling Stars

Deep upon the ocean floor, a family of starfishes dwelled among the coral. One day, as all little ones eventually do, the little one asked his mother where he came from.

Mother starfish set him down upon a reef and told him of wondrous adventures. "We come from a long way away, little son. We once lived in a sea of darkness, much like this, but far, far away."

The little starfish sat wide-eyed, one of his little pointy arms scratching his brow. "Far, far away, Mama?" he asked. "Where?"

"In the sky, my baby," she answered. "We shone like diamonds in the night, like the luminous sea creatures that dance by us on the waves. But, we shone brighter, much brighter," she whispered.

She kept her voice low because the luminous creatures had big egos and liked to think they were the brightest in the sea.

"Once we have shone for thousands and thousands of years, it is our time to fly. Some of us are afraid. Some of us burst with light and excitement when our time comes."

"Why are some afraid, Mama?" he asked. "Were you afraid?"

"Yes, I was afraid, but I kept my faith and believed that all would be all right. I had to believe, because I carried you inside me, and I would soar forever to keep you well."

"The ones who were frightened to fly did not have the faith to travel far enough in the sky over the ocean. They fell to dry ground and perished. The ones with faith soared in a blaze of light and fell to the sea, where their lives continued for eternity. Some very special horse stars (we know them as Pegasus) gallop across the sky when it is their time. They become beautiful sea horses of the ocean."

"My friend Peggy is a seahorse," the little one shouted.

"Yes," Mama answered. "One day, her mother will tell her this story as well. But for now, do not mention it. It is her mother's tale to tell, not ours."

"When people of the earth look up to the heavens, they see us. Some see us falling and make a wish. For those of us with faith, our wish is coming true, for we will live eternally in the sea."

Little starfish closed his weary eyes and gave a big yawn. It was time to sleep and dream of soaring in the sky.

Earth Angels

*I*n an ancient time when the world was new, God chose the gentlest Angels to live upon the earth.

"Do you wish to be mortals?" God asked.

"No," replied the Angels. "We wish to keep our wings. We wish to keep our voices to sing your praises. We wish to bring peace and gentleness to the earth."

God sat and pondered. He had created beautiful beasts of every size, shape, and form. Now, he set to create a winged being of such gentleness and soothing song that all mortals throughout the earth would see her as a symbol of love and peace.

"I have decided," God said.

He looked at his band of beautiful Angels, and as they flew, their wings filled with feathers, their mouths turned to beaks, and their voices changed to gentle coos.

"From this day forward, you shall be the doves of the earth. People will see you as peace, as love, as me."

With that, the band of doves flew down to earth to live among the mortals. Each early morning and each evening, one can hear their gentle coos as they sing their praise to God.

Mica

Did you ever gaze upon the earth

And see sparkles on the ground?

Men call this mineral mica

And on earth it does abound

It glistens in the sunlight

Beneath the moon it shines

Men need it to make rockets

And dig it out of mines

But first it shimmers wings

Of fairies and of fey

Giving energy for flight

Until their dying day

So, as you gaze upon the pavement

And see a sparkle to your eye.

Remember it's a fairy

Who left it as she died.

There is power in its sparkle

In its glisten and its hue

For a fairy left its beauty

When her days on earth

Were through.

Now men use it for their rockets

It helps to make them fly

But first a fairy

Soared from mica

Her wings sparkling

In the sky

Next time you see it shining

Hold it in your hand

And understand the magic

The fairies left on land

Sung from Her Heart

Once upon a time, in a green woodland pond, lived a tiny frog. He was a gentle being, with a soft peep that whispered in the starry night. He was a lonely little frog, the last of his kind on the banks of this secluded pond. Each night, he peeped his little heart out, but no one answered his calls.

Then, one night, an answer came. From high in the trees came the same peep.

"Are you a frog?" his happy frog heart murmured.

"I am a mockingbird" she replied. "Don't you know about mockingbirds?" she asked. "We can mimic the sound of most any being. Listen." And she chirped just like a cardinal. Then, she cawed just like a crow. Finally, she let out three soft peeps, just like a little frog.

The frog's heart was saddened, but he was glad to have a new friend. Each night, he peeped his sorrowful song. Each night, the mockingbird talked to him about her adventures in the woodlands.

"I have seen so many things, frog. I have seen yellow flowers as tall as tiny trees, poking their heads to the sun. I have seen trees that reach the sky, with leaves sharp like porcupine quills. I have seen creatures, huge creatures running without fur, speaking strange sounds that even I cannot mimic." Each night, she shared adventures of the north, of the south, of the east, and of the west with her friend.

"I have seen endless ponds that seem to flow forever."

"Forever?" answered the frog, his large eyes growing wider in wonder. "You saw ponds that flow forever!?!"

"Yes, forever," the mockingbird answered.

Each night, she told him stories; each night, he softly peeped. His heart longed for a little frog to call his mate, to share his lily pad, to raise a family of little tadpoles on the pond.

Each night, the mockingbird shared another little piece of her tiny heart with him, for she had fallen in love with the tiny being. She longed to nestle on his lily pad, but her nest was in the tall trees. She whispered in mockingbird song, "I love you." But he did not understand.

Frog kept thinking of mockingbird's words. *Ponds that flow forever.* If ponds were forever in this place, then a little girl frog must live there! Oh, how he wished she could find her!

One night, as the mockingbird finished her day's adventurous tale, little frog summoned up the courage and asked, "Will you help me?"

Mockingbird would do anything for little frog; she loved him.

• • •

"Will you go to the forever pond and peep like a frog for me?" he asked.

"Why?" the mockingbird answered.

"She will hear you, and she will follow. I know it," the little frog replied. "Please, mockingbird, my heart is lonely. Please find her for me."

Little mockingbird could feel her own heart cracking, for she loved little frog with all of it. "I will go to forever pond, my friend," she softly whispered, holding back the cracks in her chirps. "I will find her."

And so she did. Day after day, she flew to forever pond, calling for the frog. She hardly spent enough time looking for food, and flying so far each day had made her grow weaker and weaker.

Each night, she returned to her nest and listened for the peep of her beloved.

"Did you find her? Is she coming, mockingbird?" he asked.

"Not yet, my frog," she whispered. Her voice was softer than usual, but it was very dark. Frog could not see how her sparkling eyes seemed duller in the moonlight. "Go to sleep, my friend," she whispered. "I will find her tomorrow."

And so she did. The next morning, mockingbird set out for forever pond. She peeped and peeped. She peeped her heart out. And then, she heard her. A soft reply at first, shy and gentle. Then, stronger.

"You are not a frog!! Why do you peep like one?"

Mockingbird told her about little frog. She sang to her in the language of frogs so she would understand. "He waits," she sang. "He is a handsome prince. Go to him, and be happy."

Forever pond was beautiful, but it was lonely. But forever pond frog was very frightened of this journey away from her home.

"I will show you the way. Look up in the sky and follow me," mockingbird sang. "When the trees block your sight, listen for my song. I will guide you to him."

With that, the unlikely pair set out. The journey was long. Forever pond frog could not fly like mockingbird. What took mockingbird one day took forever pond frog several days and nights to journey.

They traveled by day and by night, with the sun and stars to guide them. Mockingbird grew weaker and weaker, but she soared above forever pond frog, guiding every step and keeping watch for any dangers.

Back at woodland pond, little frog missed his friend. He worried when she did not come home to the tree each night. Had one of the giant creatures gotten her? Had forever pond swept her away?

Several days passed. Then, early one morning, woodland frog heard a familiar peep, then another! It was the peep of a girl frog. Woodland frog cast his large eyes upon her and fell in frog love at the very first glimpse. His heart swelled in his chest and expanded three times its size! In all the excitement, he had forgotten to look up to the tree and see mockingbird.

With sorrow, the little, tired bird watched. She watched woodland frog and forever pond frog hold hands and whisper softly to one another. Her heart longed to hear those whispers.

Mockingbird felt so very tired. She could hardly hold up her tiny head. She softly chirped a tiny goodbye and fell lightly on a lily pad below. She had given her heart to a tiny frog, and without that heart, she could not go on.

Take a Walk with Me, Papa

Dartagnan was a loyal friend, disguised as a black cat with striking eyes of gold. He lived with his Papa, disguised as a two-legged human on the coast of France. But the two were kindred souls, no matter if fur or flesh surrounded bones.

Each morning, Dartagnan tapped his paw against Papa's leg. "Give me a minute, little one," Papa would answer.

Papa's legs worked slower now. If truth be told, so did the aging feline's. Walking along the cobbled paths was harder now for both of them. Papa carried a walking stick to lean on. Dartagnan had Papa's leg to rest upon when breaths came heavier.

But out the door they went. Rain, sun, wind—each day the loving pair could be seen. Each home was a beacon of light from a smiling hello or the wagging tail or nuzzling face of a furry friend.

Everyone in the village knew Papa and Dartagnan, and they knew everyone else. But years had taken their toll. Some no longer stood at the door, waiting to wave or say hello. Papa said hello anyway, even to those long gone. Luckily, Dartagnan and Papa had each other, and that was enough. As they passed each house, Papa stopped to remember.

And so did Dartagnan. He told Papa tales of each cat that he missed. Papa could not understand, but he knew. He smiled and stooped down to stroke Dartagnan's back each time the little cat stopped at familiar doors.

"I remember her, too," Papa would whisper. "Wasn't she the pretty one, with green eyes that shone like emeralds? She always waited for you, my son. Her eyes were only for you."

There was Henri's house. Henri was an excellent mouser, the very best in the village. Dartagnan idolized him, so full of feline muscle and prowess.

They passed the home of timid Pierre. Small for his age, Pierre was so afraid of Papa. He would hide under the cottage and only wave a fleeting paw of hello in Dartagnan's direction. Dartagnan could not understand why, but he knew Pierre must have suffered at the hands of a man in a cruel manner. He only trusted the women of his village.

Then, there was the tiny stone cottage where Genevieve sat each morning on the cobbled path. She was Papa's favorite. He carried special treats in his pocket for her.

So many empty houses now, not so many friends. Papa still carried those treats, but only Dartagnan got one at the end of their journey each morning.

• • •

Dartagnan felt very chilly this morning. The sun was shining brilliantly, but his body could not warm to her rays. His steps were slower. Papa noticed.

"Are you all right, my boy?" he asked. "Let us stop here and rest for a while, for I am tired too." They chose a beautiful field strewn with lavender. The man slowly eased his tired legs down, and Dartagnan nestled at his side.

"Papa!! Can you see them? They are running through the lavender. There is Henri! And Pierre! And Genevieve!!! Can you see them, Papa?"

But Papa could not see. His eyes were filled with tears as he stroked the quiet body of his little boy. He took the curved end of his walking stick and dug in the soft, lavender laden ground.

"Rest here, my loyal friend, until the day you come to walk by my side forever." From his pocket, Papa dropped a treat on top of the freshly dug earth. Deep within his heart, Papa knew there would not be too many more walks until the two were together again.

The Hare and the Wren

Once upon a time, in a dense thicket of woodland, there lived an old hare and a baby wren. The two were best friends. More than friends, they were family. The old hare loved the little bird as his son. It had been many years since hare had children of his own. But the little wren took up residence within the old hare's heart.

You might think that an odd thing, but little wren lost his parents when he was just a fledgling and found the soft fur of old hare to be a comforting blanket upon which to grow. Wise hare taught him the tender grasses of the woodland, showed him the dangers of the forest, and was a wonderful father. But he could not teach him how to fly.

The old hare was wise with years. He had danced among the wildflowers for many a spring and summer season. The little wren was just trying out his new feathers, afraid to take great "leaps" in the sky.

"Fly, little wren," cried the hare. "Do not be afraid to let the wind carry you. Once, the wind soared through my large ears and carried me through the heather. No one could catch me. In a flash of the sunbeams, I was gone from man's eyes. Now, the years have stiffened my legs, and the wind doesn't carry me as quickly anymore."

Little wren watched as hare jumped through the shrubbery. He thought him still spry and agile and wished his own tiny feet were longer so he could jump at the dandelion puffs that sailed through the air. He was happy to fly on Father Hare's back.

"No, you must learn to fly through the sky," whispered hare. "You are not of the heather. You are of the clouds. The trees are your home. My home is the warrens and hollows of the woodland floor. Your home is the sun and the moon and the stars."

Wise hare loved the moon. At night, he would gaze upon her beauty. "One day, little wren, you will fly up to her," he sighed. "You must say hello to her for me."

Little wren tried to fly. He spread his tiny feathers and gave a jump. He landed about six inches away on a patch of soft heather. "It is useless, father!" he cried. "I will never see the stars, the clouds, or the moon." With that, little wren frowned in failure.

"Why, you need an airstrip, my son. Somewhere to learn how to take off on great adventures," he added. "I will build one for you."

With those words, old hare started stomping the soft ground with his large hind feet. He began pulling out the tall grass and weeds in his mouth and setting them aside, clearing a long, straight path through the forest floor. He worked all morning, clearing and patting until many feet of earth were clear of all debris.

Wren watched with quizzical eyes as hare raced back and forth, his feet busy thumping at the earth and his mouth busy chewing at the greenery. "There!" hare exclaimed. "Start at the beginning. Here! Now start to run along the path. Let the wind lift your feathers. When you get to the finish, raise your wings into the air and fly!"

Little wren started at the beginning. He let his tiny feet run as fast as they could. He ran and ran until he was out of breath. When he got to the end of the path, he let out a sigh and dragged his tiny wings along the ground.

"I will never fly," he cried.

"Yes, you will. You just need to practice," the old hare replied.

So, practice he did. Each morning, the gentle breeze carried wren's tiny feet a little easier. Each day, his feathers puffed a bit more surely. Each day, the old hare watched with a twinkle in his eyes.

Then, one windy morning, hare twitched his nose in the breeze and smiled. He pointed his left ear to the north wind and gazed at the horizon.

"Today, I shall lose a dear friend," he whispered to himself. "I shall lose my son." Hare's heart sank within his chest, but his wise mind smiled. For hare knew what was meant to be in the world; he knew the rightful place for a little bird. "Come, my son," he cried. "Today is flying day!"

Wren raced down the path and let his feathers lift in the wind. He was soaring above the trees, he was racing after dandelion puffs, and he was watching as old hare grew tinier and tinier below him.

Old hare flapped his ears in farewell. He was wise beyond years and knew that wren would leave, must leave his side. For that was life.

His days of flying through the heather were dwindling, but for a little wren, life and flight had just begun. He had greetings from Father Hare to deliver to the moon.

My Little Black Cat

My little black cat

With her bright green eyes

Likes to sleep on my

Windowsill

May she dream of hunts

On the African plain

Instead of a fly

To kill

May my blooming rose

Against the pane

Be a woodland dense

And deep

May the falling drop

Be an Amazon rain

To lull her fast asleep

May her dreams be wild

May her soul run free

Across great paths

Unknown

Until the sound of

A spoon and can

Brings my hungry

Warrior home.

Stained Glass on a Sunny Day

Do you sometimes wonder

If we all see the same?

Each shade of blue, each hue of green

The glow of candle flame?

Do my eyes see what yours do

As they gaze upon the day?

Do my ears hear what yours hear

As we go about our way?

How can we know

I ponder

This mystery will remain

Do others see exactly?

Do others hear the same?

I think the master painters

Renoir, Van Gogh, Monet

Must have seen the colors

Always……

Like stained glass on a sunny day

Just a little brighter

Just a bit more gleam

Perhaps the hues of heaven

Shone through in each sunbeam

Yes, I often wonder

If my eyes

See the same

Or few gaze

Heaven's palette

While still on earthly plane

But when I see a stained glass window

Shining brilliant in the sun

I know the colors God made

Can be shared by everyone.

In Their Shoes

homas Thornton was having a dream, a disturbing one. He had been having a lot of them lately. There wasn't much to dream of anymore, really. Eighty-eight years had taken their toll, and his worn out body didn't pursue many adventures anymore. Usually, sleep was restful, plentiful. Sleep filled his days in his favorite chair, blocking out the world and blocking out those nearest to his heart. But now, dreams were lifting him from slumber, taking him to another place, another time.

It was dusk. A haze filled the air in Thomas's dream. He walked along a quiet path, quite peacefully. But then, a towering man blocked his steps. His stature was foreboding, but his face was not threatening and Thomas did not fear.

By the side of the path lay a pile of shoes. All types of shoes, from the sneakers of a little child to the worn work boots of a laborer. Something was oddly familiar about those shoes, but Thomas's mind felt as hazy as the air around him.

The stranger pointed to the pile and beckoned Thomas to come closer. "Pick them up," his voice bellowed. Thomas really didn't want to pick up any one of the dirty, old shoes, but there was something compelling him to do so.

His wrinkled hands reached out to the worn out work boots. Instantly, he saw him. It was his father, yelling in his face. "You will never be good enough. You are not strong like me. You cannot do the hard lifting and labor I do. You, with your nose in the books, will those books put bread upon your table? You will amount to nothing!"

The words cut through his heart like a sword; time had brought no healing to their wounds. Eighty years and he was still that hurt little boy, trying to fill the boots he was told he never could. He felt it all, heard it all. He was that fifteen-year-old boy again, never good enough, never strong enough, never deserving enough of his father's love. Thomas dropped the boots down.

"I am leaving!" he cried.

"You cannot leave, Thomas. Pick up another."

Thomas slowly stooped down and reluctantly reached for a woman's slipper. He felt comforted by this frayed, fuzzy piece of cloth. Then, he saw her, his mother. He felt her pain; he felt her disappointment in life. He felt her trapped in a house with an abusive husband. He saw through her eyes, looking at a young boy with love and sorrow, feeling even more trapped by his presence. He felt her love, but he felt all the rest that dwelled in her heart and why she could never fully open her heart to his. Thomas dropped the slippers.

"Who are you?" he asked the stranger. "What is this place?" he cried.

The stranger handed Thomas a tiny pair of sneakers. They had little action figures on the sides. Thomas recognized them; he had taught the little boy how to tie their laces. His son.

Thomas saw the little boy, tears running down his face. Thomas heard his stern voice yelling at the child. "Throw the ball this way. Hold the mitt like this. No, that is not good enough! Why are you so stupid? Can't you follow any directions!"

Sadly, Thomas heard his father in his voice. His pain was his son's. Such a sorrow filled his heart with regrets.

The last pair of shoes waited—a pair of sandals. Thomas knew they belonged to his wife.

"I have had enough of this game or test or whatever this is!!!" he cried. "Take your shoes and leave me alone."

Thomas tried to wake himself up. He couldn't. "Please, let the morning sun rise and stir me from this nightmare," he whispered to himself.

He looked down at his hands. The sandals were there. He felt the sorrow, the loneliness, the despair within them. He heard the sobbing, he saw the eyes of a frightened little boy watching from the top of the stairs as the arguments and hateful words flew about the room. Thomas fell to the ground.

"I am so sorry," he cried. "I am so very sorry. I must get up and tell them so. Please let me wake from this," he pleaded. "I have to tell them how sorry I am. I have to tell them I love them. Please!!"

The morning sun filled the stark room. The monitor blinked its heart rate information. Thomas' wife and grown son sat by his bedside.

"Will he regain consciousness?" his son asked as the nurse entered the hospital room.

"It is not in our hands anymore," she answered. "Please step outside and get some breakfast," she told the two of them. "I have to change the linens and wash the patient now."

She called in an orderly to help her. "Nurse James," the orderly called. "His eyes, they are crying."

"Just tearing up," she said. "Take a warm washcloth and wash his face," she directed.

The orderly took a warm cloth and washed his face, chest, and bare feet, then put on a fresh pair of hospital socks. The time was 7:05.

At 7:20, Thomas took his last steps in the dream and his last breaths on earth.

At 9:40, Thomas' son collected his father's clothes and put them in his hospital bag. He bent down beside the bed and picked up his father's shoes that were on the floor. His father's shoes would remain empty, but his son's heart was filled with sorrow and regret.

"I wish I could have told him how sorry I was that I never measured up," he sobbed. "I wish I could have told him how much I loved him. I hope he loved me."

He walked to the elevator, carrying more than the weight of empty shoes in his hands and heart.

A Happy Heart

*a*nnabelle was a cow. She lived her life on Mayfield's dairy farm. She had many, many children but saw none of them grow. Always, shortly after they were born, they were taken away in a large truck by Farmer Mayfield.

Annabelle cried each time, but no one listened. She searched all over the farm each time, but her babies never returned.

Farmer Mayfield treated Annabelle like a cow, just a cow. But Annabelle had a heart; she had a beautiful smile, and all she ever wanted from life was to be a mom and moo a song for her babies. She mooed to them while they grew inside her. Now, she was heavy with another little one. Maybe Farmer Mayfield would let this one stay. Oh, how Annabelle's heart wished to moo her little baby to sleep on the hay in the barn each night.

Little Winston came into the world late one night. Farmer Mayfield seemed annoyed to be kept up at such a late hour. But Annabelle did not have an easy birth. She was getting older and heard the doctor tell the dairy farmer she might not recover.

Annabelle needed to be strong; she needed to sing to her little boy. With all her strength, she gave birth to the tiny calf. He snuggled up to her and nestled his fuzzy, warm head onto her waiting breast. Annabelle had a happy heart. Now they both slept. She had no strength to sing a lullaby this moonlit night. Tomorrow, she would teach him all the songs she knew.

But Winston was not at her side in the morning. Panicked, Annabelle started screaming loud moos. But no one listened. Other cows came to comfort her. They told her that Winston left in the big truck again. Annabelle could not be comforted. She rose up and used all her strength to search the far end of the farm for him, mooing and mooing. No one listened.

Winston was so little and so scared. The farmer had scooped him up that morning while his mother slept and tossed him in the back of the truck with several other little calves.

"Where are we going?" he asked. But no one listened. They were all too frightened. Then, there was a loud crash. An accident left the big truck overturned, in need of repair on the roadside. Some calves didn't make it. Others started running through the fields. Winston started running.

"Mama, mama!" he mooed. Filled with terror, he started running through the tall grass with the other frightened calves.

He ran and ran and soon it became dark. No other little calves were beside him anymore. They had been rounded up and taken onto another waiting big truck. But not Winston.

The little calf hid in the field as the sun rose each day. As moonlit shone, he traveled through farmers' fields and tall grass, feeling very thirsty and hungry. He was listening. Somewhere in the distance, he could hear his mama mooing. He listened all night and walked toward her.

Annabelle cried all night, her moos echoing in the silence. She thought no one was listening. She walked wearily, without much strength in her body left, to the edge of the farm and bellowed at the fence for all the babies she had lost, especially for little Winston.

Winston listened. It took him two moons to find her. When Annabelle saw his little body slowly walking, she did what any mother would do. With every last ounce of strength, she rammed the farmer's fence and went to him. Together, under the moon, they slept.

Annabelle softly sang him all the lullabies she knew, all the lullabies she had saved for each tiny baby she had lost. She sang her heart out. For every lullaby she emptied from it, happiness swelled inside its beating chambers. Winston listened, his tiny heart filled with love and comfort.

They say one can die from a broken heart, but two happy hearts left the sorrow of being just cows that moonlit night. While on his morning chores, Farmer Mayfield found them. For a moment, he was awestruck at the lifeless pair. Only for a moment, though, for they were just cows after all.

"Oh, great!" he muttered angrily to himself. "Now I will have to repair that fence!"

If only his heart would listen………..

The Key

The Irish woods hold many treasures for those whose eyes believe. And so it was when Annie walked one late afternoon on her way home from market. The setting sun cast glimmers on the forest floor, and Annie's eyes saw a gleam amongst the moss and leaves. Bending down, she saw a beautifully shaped key, adorned with colored jewels. Amethysts, emeralds, sapphires, and diamonds studded the slender handle of this beautiful golden piece.

"This must be worth a fortune," she sighed to herself.

"Yes," a tiny voice answered. "But not near the fortune held behind the door's lock which this key opens."

Annie squinted in the dwindling sunlight and saw a tiny person. The wee folk were respected and feared in her village. Annie's heart thumped, and she quickly dropped the key onto the woodland floor.

"Do not fear, my child. The key is yours. You may sell it now or find the treasure that waits upon its turning. Find the lock that fits this key, and you will be richer than your wildest dreams." With that, the tiny man vanished in the leaves.

Annie tucked the key inside her pocket and ran home. Her life was hard, barely any food to place upon her table and barely enough money to get by each winter. And winter was approaching.

What should she do? She was sure this key would fetch a handsome price in the village. But how could she explain where it came from? She knew revealing it would open much more than a secret door; her quiet life would never be the same. The woods would be filled with treasure seekers, searching for the wee folk.

That night, the fire of her hearth caught the gleam of the stones as she gazed upon the key. Annie thought to herself. "The handle of the key will not affect which lock it opens. I shall take one stone out of the handle and use it to buy food." With a sharp knife, Annie pried the stone loose from the key's handle.

The next morning, she carried it into the village and went to the wealthy merchant's shop. "How much will you give me for this beautiful purple stone?" she asked.

The merchant cleverly tried to close his gaping jaw. "It is a pretty stone," he answered. "But so many flaws. Too bad. If it were perfect, I could give you such a handsome price." Silently, the greedy merchant was in awe; he had never seen such an exquisite amethyst before. He offered Annie enough to buy a week's worth of grain and potatoes. Annie sold the stone and went home.

• • •

On the way, a tiny voice whispered from the leaves. "You have been cheated," he warned. "That amethyst was perfect. The merchant lied to you. Next time, be smarter, my friend."

The week passed, and Annie's grain dwindled. By the light of her hearth fire, she took out her little knife and pried the sapphire free. The next morning, she went to see the merchant again.

"My, that is such a beautiful stone. Too bad it isn't perfect," he began.

With that, Annie grasped the stone and said, "It *is* perfect! If you want it, you shall pay dearly for it!"

The merchant had never seen such a lovely shade of blue. And pay dearly for it, he did.

Annie had money now to buy beautiful gowns, delicious sweets, and all the finery a wealthy woman could desire. She abandoned her little cottage, stopping by only to pick up the key she had hidden beneath her floorboards.

"Are you happy now?" a familiar voice whispered.

"Yes, so happy!" Annie cried.

She bought a house in town and filled it with treasures. There were luxurious laces and finely woven woolens and fancy crystal goblets in her cupboards. But truth be told, Annie was not happy. She missed her quiet life. She never used to worry about anyone coming to steal from her. There was nothing they would want. Now, she slept restlessly, her knife at her side, wary of any noise in the night.

Annie went to the village locksmith. "I wish a key made for my door," she said.

The locksmith came by and studied Annie's front door lock. "This is a very unusual door," he muttered. "I don't have tools to make a key for this intricate a design. I am sorry, but I cannot make a key for you."

Dismayed, Annie let her fears overwhelm her happiness. She withdrew from the world, afraid if she left her beautiful home, someone would come in and take it all away from her. She never walked in the lovely woodlands; she never felt the warm Irish sun on her face. Her food was delivered to her door. Money and her beautiful things were all she had. She tied her magickal key around her neck, hidden inside her clothing. Fear of losing it consumed her life.

Talented carpenters and locksmiths were hired to change the door, change the lock. But each time work began, something terrible happened; accidents would occur. Soon, word spread around the countryside. No craftsmen would take on Annie's work.

Months went by, then years. Annie grew more and more alone and unhappy. No joy filled her eyes as she looked upon her possessions. Water tasted no better out of a crystal goblet than her old wooden cup. Her fine lace shawls kept her heart no warmer than her tattered wool homespun ones had done.

One day, a tiny voice emerged from her windowsill. It was a familiar voice. Annie parted the fine lace curtains, now filled with dust. She never opened them anymore; no light filtered inside the room or inside her lonely heart.

"Annie, are you happy?" the little man asked.

Annie began to cry. The golden key around her neck became very hot, so hot she had to lift it from beneath her clothes.

"Take the key, Annie, and go home," the little man cried. "Your treasure has always been waiting."

Puzzled, Annie did what she had not done in several years. She stepped outside. The brightness hurt her eyes. But the warm Irish wind felt so wonderful against her face. Her handcrafted shoes hurt, and Annie tossed them aside. She continued on barefoot, the soft moss and bed of leaves cushioning her steps.

She came upon her old cottage. It was so tiny and quiet, but it looked so inviting to Annie's eyes. Wildflowers had sprung up in the fields surrounding it, birds sang in the trees beside it, and wild rabbits danced in the meadow.

Annie went to the front door. It would not open! Suddenly, a tiny voice whispered from the grass.

"Unlock your treasure, Annie. It has been waiting for you to come home."

Annie took the golden key and broke the cord that hung around her neck. She placed the key inside the lock and turned. The door opened. Annie was home.

What became of the key, she did not know. It had disappeared from the lock the moment she used it. As she looked about the grass, she thought she saw it glimmering in the hands of a tiny wee man as he ran away laughing.

Fairy Mouse

Priscilla was a little fairy mouse. Fairy mice are quite rare, so rare, in fact, that only the fairies catch a glimpse of their shimmering wings scampering among the blossoms. Fairy mice love flowers. Each morning, in the light of dawn, they drink the sweet nectar from tiny blossoms and begin their day.

Priscilla was a very special fairy mouse. She was extra tiny. The fairies adored her. In fact, fairy mice were the pets of the fairy folk; just like our own pets, they are dearly loved and cared for. Every once in a while, a little fairy mouse comes along that carries a very special kind of energy and is loved far more than all the others. Priscilla was like that. Her loving kindness was very strong, but her tiny body wasn't. The fairies took extra care of her, but they knew she would not live long. Sometimes, the pets we love the most leave us the soonest. The fairies knew that one day soon, their hearts would break.

Each day, they brought Priscilla special treats. Hollowed acorns became gift baskets, laden with the sweetest herbs and flowers of the fields. They brought the silkiest thistle blooms to weave a pillow for her little mouse head and the softest moss to make a blanket for her bed.

Priscilla lived in a little hole in an ancient tree. Her fragile wings could only lift her for a moment. She wished she could fly up to the tallest branches like her fairy friends. Each day, the fairies asked what they could bring to make her day extra special. Priscilla asked for one thing—she dearly loved the flowers and wished she had the strength to visit each and every one. She wanted to see each petal, smell each fragrance, but all she could do was listen to the fairies describe each one. Sometimes, they brought her a little fallen petal, which Priscilla neatly laid upon her soft moss bed.

The summer season was fading, and so was Priscilla's strength. She barely rose from her tree nest anymore. The fairies knew it would be their special friend's last summer; it would be her last time to scamper among the flowers, her last time to drink their nectar.

"We must do something very special for her," they whispered. The fairies huddled their tiny wings together and thought up a plan. It would take a lot of work, but Priscilla was worth it. And so they began.

The next morning, the fairies set upon the woodlands, collecting as many different wildflowers as their eyes beheld. They flew to the very tops of the ancient tree, holding the blossoms and bits of moss in their tiny hands. They gently wove the blossoms into the branches, being ever so gentle as to not bruise their petals. They worked all day as Priscilla slept, before the blossoms closed their heads for the evening. By nightfall, there were hundreds of blossoms of every fragrance, size, and color among the leaves.

Then, the elder fairy flew to meet a very special being of the forest. "Hello, Father Owl," he whispered.

"Why are you out so late in the dark?" the wise owl hooted.

"I have come to ask a favor, for you are a strong, wise owl," the fairy answered.

The fairy told him of the gentle mouse. Now owls aren't the best friends of mice, but in this magical woodland, all the beings were friends.

"Before you go to sleep for the day, may you grace us with one favor?" asked the elder fairy.

"What might that be?" asked the owl.

"In the early morning, would you rest in the very top boughs of the ancient tree?" the fairy answered.

"Yes, I know the tree, but why?" hooted the wise owl.

"You shall see," the little fairy answered before flitting off to sleep.

The very next morning, as the sun rose in the sky, all the fairy folk gathered around the ancient tree. They called to Priscilla. "Priscilla, please come outside for just a moment," they asked.

Priscilla was very weak, but she loved the fairy folk and took a gingerly mouse step outside. Her little fairy mouse eyes squinted in the sunlight. Just then, a loud rustle of leaves was overhead. Wise owl was landing on the ancient tree to fall asleep for the day. His huge wings caused a strong breeze to flow through ancient tree's branches, loosening all the moss tied around the flowers. As fairy mouse looked up, a shower of blossoms fell around her.

"It's raining flowers!!!!" she cried. Fairy mouse had never seen such a sight. She could see the colors drifting down around her little mouse whiskers. She could smell the perfumed blossoms drifting by her little mouse nose. Her little fairy mouse heart swelled with joy.

It really was raining that day. Not just with flowers, but with tears. As the fairies sat amongst the branches, their tears fell down upon the blossoms like morning dew. Then, wise owl and Priscilla settled down to sleep, he among the boughs and she beneath a blanket of woodland flowers.

When summer ended, Priscilla was wrapped inside her flower laden moss blanket and laid to rest beneath the ancient tree.

Follow the Moon

Once upon a time there lived a little woodland hare. He loved the moon. At night, he sat motionless in the tall grass and gazed at her in wonder. As night ceased, the little hare tried to follow the moon, but she always disappeared before his eyes.

"Where do you go?" he wondered. Little Hare asked the wise black raven. "Wise Raven, do you know where the moon goes?" he asked.

Wise Raven looked at Little Hare with his black, piercing eyes and said, "She goes far above the stars and sleeps until dark."

Little Hare's brown eyes grew wide in wonder. "Beyond the stars!?!" he cried.

"Yes, too far for my wings to carry me," answered the raven.

Little Hare came upon a sly fox in the woods. "Mr. Fox, do you know where the moon goes?"

"Why, yes," said the fox. "She travels to the distant mountains and rests upon the highest peak. It is too high for me to climb."

"The mountains?" cried Little Hare. "I shall never follow her there."

Each night, he gazed upon her light, dreaming of the place she drifted when sunlight came. Each friend along the way was asked the same question by the inquisitive hare, "Where does the moon go?"

Mother Raccoon thought she slept beneath the river; she had seen her gently lower her light upon it. Little Hare didn't want to imagine that. He hated the water. He could never follow the moon there. He didn't even like to get his big feet wet.

Simon Sparrow said there was a big hole in the sky, and moon hid herself inside each day.

"I will never find her," worried Little Hare.

Each night, he watched and waited, keeping one eye pointed to the moon. Each night, she slipped behind the clouds and disappeared.

"Why do you want to follow the moon?" the hare's friends asked.

Little Hare tried to explain, but his woodland friends just didn't understand his dreams.

One day, Little Hare came upon a strange creature. He did not have fur, he walked on two legs, and he spoke in strange sounds.

"Do you know where the moon goes?" asked the hare.

The furless being did not understand, but he smiled at the hare and continued on his way.

Little Hare told his friends, and they warned him to stay away. This was a man, and those of his kind were not always a friend.

But Little Hare didn't listen and quietly crept in the bushes until he reached the spot where the man was sleeping. Little Hare's long leg made a twig snap, and the man stirred from his slumber. He reached for a stick and held it in his hands. A bright beam glowed in the darkness!

"The moon!" the hare cried. "He has captured the moon!!!" Little Hare sat, quiet as a fallen log. He watched the man shine the moon around the bushes. Then, he put her down and went back to sleep.

Little Hare took tiny steps closer and closer to the moon. He picked her up and carried her off to his friends, running as fast as his long legs could carry him.

"I have followed her!!!" he cried.

Sly Fox picked up the stick. "This is not the moon!" he laughed. He fumbled with the stick, and his paws moved a piece on its side. Suddenly, a brilliant beam glowed.

"The moon!" Mother Raccoon shrieked. "Hare has found her!"

Sly Fox dropped the stick and ran off, trembling in the bushes.

Wise Raven perched on a branch, the beam of light glistening in his coal black eyes.

Little Hare picked up the stick and shone it in the sky. From that day on, he was known as the hare who followed and found the moon.

Christmas Eve Snow

 esley didn't fit in. From kindergarten through high school, she was the loner. The strange one. The one you didn't talk to, the one you didn't invite to your lunch table, the one with whom no notes were tossed across the hall while changing classes.

That was okay with Leslie. She had her books, her artwork, her spirits. Yes, Lesley talked to spirits. They would seek her out; she would help them in any way she could. Now that high school was over, the world was waiting. But it is tough venturing out into a world in which you never really belonged.

Lesley read stories, myths and legends about sacred sites and gifted healers persecuted throughout lifetimes. She shared a bond with these souls; she knew that if centuries were different, she would be one of them.

She thought about moving away from her hometown. She loved her parents, but they, too, were mystified by a daughter's abilities they couldn't fully understand. Things were kept secret, as though pushing them under the carpet would eliminate them from reality.

College? She probably wouldn't fit in there either. Parties and sororities weren't her cup of tea, and finding a roommate would be an impossible task.

So Lesley's thoughts turned to escape. She would find a place where she would fit. Salem? No, too touristy and filled with "wannabe" witches and psychics. Lesley had her fill of them in the town's metaphysical shop. So many claiming powers and spells. But Lesley knew that the genuinely gifted were few and far between.

Money wasn't an issue. Lesley had true artistic talent. She often set up her easel on the town corner and painted portraits. The local art gallery had even hosted a showing of her work, quite an achievement for one so young.

So where? Lesley glanced over to her bookshelf and realized the one place to which her heart had always been drawn—Pendle Hill, England, the legendary home of the Pendle Witches. A place of quietness, not like the busy streets of Salem. A place for an artist to paint the sullen landscapes and not have to bear the judging faces of those around her.

Lesley left the week after high school ended. She left with no set direction, except to go where the winds of destiny and perhaps some guiding spirits led her.

When her feet set upon the earth of Pendle Hill, she knew she was home. There were tourist shops here, and she set about asking for employment and shelter. High on a windy hill, Lesley came upon a tiny witch shop. Filled with touristy kitchen witches and crystals, Lesley was at first hesitant to step inside. But a friendly voice carried through the open door into the Pendle air.

"Come in, child. Why has fate summoned you to my door?"

Lesley saw a plump, middle-aged woman with brilliant red hair and an easy smile beckon her inside with crooked fingers.

"I am looking for work, and maybe a place to stay," Lesley answered.

"Well now! It seems you have come to the perfect spot. I have been needing an assistant around here. The tourist buses come at all hours, and my aging bones are finding it hard to start the morning early or end the day late."

Lesley couldn't help but look around. She saw a lot of spirits in the shop. From the way the woman looked at her, she sensed she could see them, too.

"Don't worry, they're friends. Just need a place to fit in, too," she whispered with a smile. "So, do you want the job? There's a tiny room in back. Not much, but cozy when the harsh Pendle Hill winds blow. No rent—that is part of your salary. I can't pay much here; tourists like to come out of curiosity, but not many buy. I hardly eke out a living here."

Like a wandering boat on the ocean, Lesley was adrift. For some reason, this woman felt like an anchor in her storm.

"My name's Hermione. What's yours?"

"Lesley. Lesley Warner."

"Welcome, Lesley Warner. How about some tea?"

That late June, a friendship blossomed like the summer flowers on Pendle Hill. Hermione saw herself in the young girl. She understood the loneliness. Soon, Lesley became a daughter to her. And it was so nice for Lesley, too, to have someone who saw the same things she did and not someone with whom pretending to be normal was the only way to keep peace.

Soon, Lesley knew each kitchen witch price, each Pendle Hill magnet, each knick-knack and corner of the shop. And all the while, she painted. Lovely scenes. People started noticing and coming in for her artwork. The two of them were getting by—no, better than getting by—succeeding. Hermione knew she had found capable hands.

One night, as they closed the shop, Hermione grasped Lesley's hand. "I have something I wish to tell you," she whispered. "It has been several months since you came here," she added. "You may have the shop now if you wish it."

"What?" Lesley asked. "What do you mean? This is your shop."

"Yes," Hermione answered. "But I have let so much in life pass by. And life is passing quickly now. I want to see what else awaits me before it is too late. I came to this place as a young girl too. Now, I am not so young anymore. I let too many Decembers pass by. It is autumn now in Pendle, and autumn now in my life. You are more than capable to steer ship here. I will write you from all my adventures. Now it is time for you to begin yours."

Hermione had a twinkle in her eye, a twinkle that usually came when spirits were afoot.

So, on a brisk November day, Hermione left the shop. She left Lesley sole management; she left her the bigger apartment above the small room; she left a lifetime of hopes and dreams in a young girl's hands.

As she crossed the threshold of the shop, Hermione added, "Welcome Thomas. He comes on Christmas Eve, but only when it snows. Tell him I have gone to live out my dreams."

Lesley looked quizzically at her friend, but Hermione hurried to meet the waiting taxi with a wave of her arm as she quickly got in the passenger door.

December came. Weather was unusually cold in Pendle Hill. Weather reports called for a snowy Christmas. The shop was bustling; Lesley's paintings were selling as briskly as the winds. She had forgotten about Hermione's goodbye words.

Christmas Eve. The snow was falling gently on the hill. Lesley closed up shop—no more last minute buyers. Time to have a quiet Christmas by her cozy fire. Suddenly, a knock on the shop door startled her. Who could be out at this hour? Another last minute shopper perhaps?

Lesley opened and saw the most beautiful man she had ever seen. Long brown locks caressed his shoulders, and his black eyes shone like coals.

"Hermione?" he called. "Hermione, where are you?"

Lesley remembered. "Thomas?" she asked.

"Yes, I am Thomas Wickham. Where is my friend?"

"She has gone to live out her dreams."

Thomas smiled. "Well, it is high time," he answered with a laugh.

Then he looked at Lesley. Her beauty was astounding. There was something else, a knowing, a belonging he felt as he gazed into her eyes. "May I stay for the night?" he asked. "My horse cannot travel in the snow. I have put him in the barn out back, for I thought Hermione was here. Is it all right? We often stayed here on snowy eves. And my hound, as well."

Lesley looked out in the snow and saw an enormous wolfhound sitting, his tongue hanging out, panting from wearily galloping in the snow. "Yes, you are welcome. Please come in." With that, she gestured for Thomas to call his hound inside.

• • •

There was something strange about Thomas. She was so in awe of his beauty that it had dulled her other senses. It took a while before she realized the truth. She realized the reason for his odd clothes, for his mode of transportation on this snowy night, and for the way the hound moved stealthily without even as much as a click of his nails on her wooden floor.

"Thomas, who are you?" she asked.

"Someone who lived here many years ago. My father's land was just over that ridge," he replied. "That was a long time ago, centuries past. All is gone now, my home, my life, the 1800s."

"We wander these hills on snowy Christmas eves, my horse, hound, and I, on the night of our accident, seeking shelter when none had been given so long ago. We had almost reached home, but the snow was so deep. We were so near, but so far away, too far to make it home again. And so we wandered. We wandered for centuries, until a gifted one like you found us."

"Hermione saw us. She knew us. You do, too. You remind me of her. Please tell her she will always be a friend."

And so Lesley, Thomas, and the hound shared a warm place and hot tea by the fire. At the strike of midnight, Thomas held a tiny box in his hand and gave it to Lesley.

"For Christmas," he whispered. Lesley opened it, and inside was a lovely hair comb. "For your lovely hair."

Lesley lifted her locks in an upsweep and pushed the comb in place. "Thank you," she whispered.

With dawn's light, Thomas walked to the barn and climbed on his horse. With hound at his side, they vanished over the ridge.

Lesley couldn't get his face or his voice out of her mind. But he was gone. Hermione sent a letter. *I heard it snowed there on Christmas Eve. Have you met Thomas?* Lesley read. *I knew the two of you were meant to be,* wrote Hermione. *Remember, only on snowy Christmas Eves. Treasure them. Don't let your chances pass by.*

Lesley was uncertain of her friend's words, but business kept her thoughts occupied. She had so many portrait commissions to complete. At night, she worked on personal paintings, recreating the beautiful face, the long brown locks, the coal black eyes ever present in her memories. She showed no one these, but rather kept them locked in a back storeroom.

A couple of years passed. Hermione traveled the globe. Letters and silk from China and lovely bamboo brushes (with which to paint), spices, and teas from India fragranced her letters home to Lesley.

No snow for the next two winters. Then, Christmas Eve was white again. Lesley closed the shop early, her heart eagerly awaiting her spirit visitor. And right on cue, the knocks came.

She flew to the door and reached out her arms to welcome Thomas, who looked exactly the same. Again, they shared their Christmas Eve together, traveler, hound, and horse (safely tied up in the barn).

This year, Thomas had a large parcel tied on his saddlebag. He undid the ties and gave the package to Lesley. She opened it, and the softest, warmest hooded cloak unfurled before her eyes.

"Oh, it is so lovely."

"No match for your loveliness," Thomas answered. With that, he gave her a kiss. Lesley's heart pounded.

The night flew too fast. Soon the morning approached, and Thomas headed for the door.

"Please, don't go," she cried.

"I must. I don't belong here," he answered. "One day, you will decide where you belong, as Hermione did," he added. With those words, he vanished.

More seasons, more tourists, more paintings. Lesley was happy, but her thoughts strayed never far from Thomas.

With him, she belonged. "I must tell him," she whispered to herself.

Not for three more years did snow finally grace Pendle Hill on December 24. Thomas came, and together they spent the few hours fate had given.

"I want to go with you, Thomas," she cried.

"You must be sure. I leave you this special gift this Christmas, my love. Do not open it until I am gone."

The next morning, Lesley undid the beautiful bow and found a ring. The top of the ring had a clasp that opened to reveal a powdery substance. Leslie placed the top back on, closed the clasp, and tucked the ring safely away in her wooden jewelry chest.

The very next December, snow came to the Hill. A deep snowstorm. Lesley kept the shop closed. She placed all her finished commissions neatly on the shelf with each person's name and phone number attached. Then, she went to her bedroom with a cup of tea, put on her beautiful cloak, fashioned her hair in a lovely upsweep with her comb, and took her ring box out of the chest. She poured the powder into her tea and drank it. Then, she placed the ring on her finger.

Days passed. The shop wasn't open. Those who had commissioned paintings began to worry. They called the police to investigate.

Hermione received a telegram in Australia. *Shop closed. Looks like the shopkeeper took her own life. Sad situation. Please come home to settle affairs.*

Hermione took the next flight home. She entered the shop and saw all the commissioned paintings with notes attached. Then, she took out her storeroom key and unlocked the latch. There sat several paintings of a familiar face. A face she once had loved. A man she could never summon courage enough to follow until too many years had passed by.

Then, she saw the last painting, still on the easel, not entirely dry. It showed a distant horse and hound, a man and a cloaked woman riding together, snow falling all around them. It was signed *Lesley Wickham, 1840.*

"Strange signature, don't you think?" the policeman asked. "And so sad, a young woman ending her life before any of her dreams could be lived," he added.

Hermione just nodded, a wistful twinkle in her eye as she stepped outside in the winter snow.

"Will you be closing the shop now, Ma'am?" the officer asked.

"Perhaps," she sighed. "Then again, maybe I will wait for one final Pendle Christmas snow. So lovely, don't you think? Just like a fairy tale."

Nantucket Valentine

Emily lived on Nantucket Island. Nineteen years of age and engaged to handsome James O'Malley, Emily lived for the day James could save enough money to build their little cottage. A small plot of land at the northern end of the island, given to the couple by Emily's father, stood waiting for that day.

James was a gifted carpenter; none could make a joint seal as water tight as O'Malley. But carpentry jobs didn't bring in the money. A stint on a whaling ship paid, so James signed on.

Emily's heart was filled with dread. She watched the whaling widows stroll the walks and gaze out to sea, hoping for a speck of a whaling ship to enter the horizon. Who knew how long James would be away—months, years?

"Don't go, Jim. We can wait and save up longer," she cried.

"No, Emily, I want to make you my wife now, not later. And that great whale is going to help me do it."

So, on a foggy morning, Emily watched her dreams disappear on the waves. She spent her days weaving for her hope chest and waiting for a letter, any letter carried from a distant port by a seafaring messenger back to Nantucket.

Each morning, she walked to the far point of the Island, where a lighthouse stood to guide seafaring men back to shore. She climbed the rocks, watching the sea and the seals playing in the shimmering sunlit waves. Emily loved the seals. "Send a message to my love," she called to them. "Tell James I am waiting." The seals seemed to follow Emily as though they knew her loneliness, why she waited on the rocks each day.

Each afternoon, she walked to the harbor, waiting for all ships that came in that day. Each ship that docked, each band of seamen who departed, was asked the same question, "Have you seen *The Grey Lady*? Do you have news of her crew?" And each answer echoed the same head shaking response.

The sea was rough. James had little time to spare, but when he did, he wrote a few lines more in a lengthy letter to his waiting love. By moonlight, he created a tiny wooden chest with a heart carved onto the lid. Inside the heart, he carved the name Emily. He glued tiny shells around the heart shape, a pastime many sailors took part in called a sailor's valentine. These were made for those waiting back home, those who were terribly missed on the lonely seas.

As he worked in the quiet of the night, he watched the seal heads pop above the water. He laughed and talked to them as they followed the whaling ship. "Seals, swim the waves back to Nantucket Isle, for there is a pretty girl named Emily waiting for me there. Tell her I love her and when I come home, she will be my bride." And James laughed as he saw the seals swim off toward Nantucket, wishing he could join them.

Finally, a whale was sighted, a massive creature. James knew all on board were needed, so he tucked his letter inside the valentine chest and went on deck to lend a hand. Unfortunately, *The Grey Lady* lost her battle; she went down with the wounded whale.

Months passed back on Nantucket. No letters from James. Emily's heart grew heavier and heavier. Each day, none but the seals saw her weeping on the rocks, and none but the seals heard her crying on the shore.

Then, one morning, a group of seals raised heads above the waves where Emily watched. They pushed a tiny wooden box to the shoreline. Emily picked it up. Her name was carved into the top and tiny shells, some broken now, adorned the lid. Emily gasped. She opened the lid. Inside she found a letter:

Dearest Emily,

My heart hopes to see your face smile as you see this valentine, but if the fates don't permit it, may a kind friend deliver it to you for me. The sea is very rough. I have little time to write, but what time I have, I will put my heart into these words for you.

I have many friends here, and many of them live in the sea. It makes me sad to think I have come on this voyage to kill one of them. The seals follow us, Emily. I talk to them at night and tell them to visit you. You will think me sea crazy, my love, but I know they understand.

Emily read each line until the last hurried words before James took his place on deck to fight the whale. She knew *The Grey Lady* met her fate at the bottom of the waves, taking James and his valentine along with her.

Emily tossed the letter to the sea. She unwrapped her shawl, placed it on the rocks, and slowly walked into the waves, the wooden valentine in her hands.

"Take me to him," she cried to the seals.

And they did. They carried Emily's still body to the bottom of the sea, where James lay at rest among the shells. They placed her beside her love, his sailor's valentine on her heart.

Epilogue

I have a tall pine tree in my yard. Her energy has crossed; her withered trunk no longer flows with any life source. But she is surrounded by life. Very old ivy climbs her boughs and now blossoms and berries. It takes ivy a very long time to blossom. Most people don't know that it does. But after a life of many seasons, she fills the harvest time with nourishment for the swarms of bees around her.

I like to think life is like this. After many years, I hope people still provide nourishment and wisdom in the final years of blossom and berry.

This is my fourth collection of fairy tales. I set out to write one, then two, and then my next two found their way onto the page. In my later years, the time when imagination and fairy tales wither for most, I have set upon a quest to recapture them for young and old alike once more. I hope you have enjoyed this collection.

Wishing you many seasons of enchanted lives,
Shirl